Scholastic's The Magic School Bus®

HOPS HOME
A Book About Animal Habitats

SCHOLASTIC INC.
New York   Toronto   London   Auckland   Sydney

Based on the episode from the animated TV series
produced by Scholastic Productions, Inc.
Based on *The Magic School Bus* book series
written by Joanna Cole and illustrated by Bruce Degen.

TV tie-in book adaptation by Patricia Relf and illustrated by Nancy Stevenson.
TV script written by Ronnie Krauss, Brian Meehl, and Jocelyn Stevenson.

ISBN 0-590-48413-3

Copyright © 1995 by Scholastic Inc.
All rights reserved. Published by Scholastic Inc.
SCHOLASTIC and THE MAGIC SCHOOL BUS
are registered trademarks of Scholastic Inc.

Library of Congress Cataloging-in-Publication Data

Relf, Patricia.
Scholastic's The magic school bus hops home: a book about animal
habitats / from an episode of the animated TV series produced by
Scholastic Productions, Inc.; based on the Magic school bus books
written by Joanna Cole and illustrated by Bruce Degen.
p. cm.
"TV tie-in book adaptation by Pat Rolf and illustrated by Nancy
Stevenson, TV script written by Jocelyn Stevenson"—T.p. verso.
ISBN 0-590-48413-3
1. Habitat (Ecology)—Juvenile literature. [1. Animals.
2. Habitat (Ecology) 3. Ecology.] I. Cole, Joanna.
II. Stevenson, Nancy W., ill. III. Scholastic Productions.
IV. Title. V. Title: Magic school bus hops home.
QH541.14.R44 1995
591.5—dc20   94-25969
                                                           CIP
                                                           AC

25 24 23 22 21 20 19 18 17 16   7 8 9/9 0/0

Printed in the U.S.A.   24
First Scholastic printing, February 1995

Ms. Frizzle is the strangest teacher in our school—and it's not just because she wears such weird clothes. . . .

Last week, we were learning about animal homes. Everything was normal until Wanda brought her best friend, Bella the bullfrog, to school.

"Wonderful!" said Ms. Frizzle. "What does a bullfrog need in her home or habitat?"

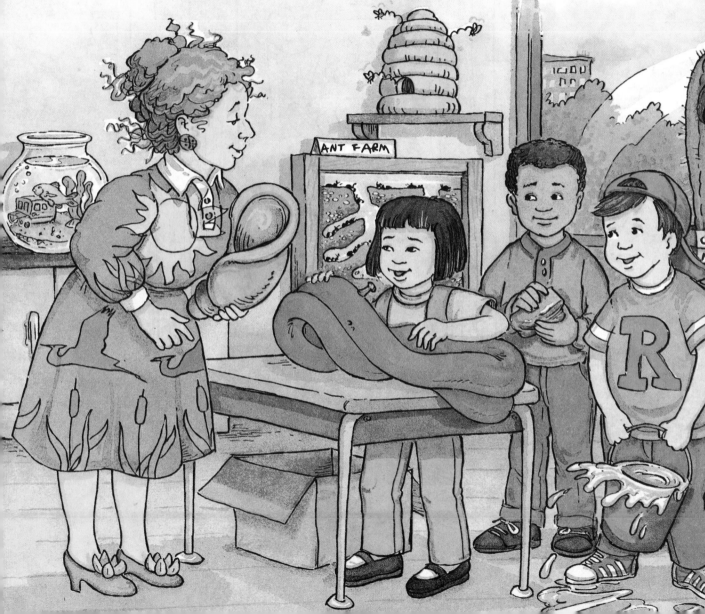

"A safe place to sleep!" said Wanda.
"Water!" said Ralphie.
"Food!" said Dorothy Ann.
"Fresh air!" said Arnold as he opened the window.

While we were making a habitat for Bella, she hopped out the window.

"*Bella!*" wailed Wanda. "Arnold, you let her get away! Ms. Frizzle, may Arnold and I go look for Bella?"

A funny gleam came into Ms. Frizzle's eyes. "Good idea, Wanda!" she said.

"Let's all look for Bella! Class, it's time for a field trip!" said the Friz as she marched us out the door.

"I *knew* it," groaned Arnold. "Another one of Ms. Frizzle's crazy field trips!"

But he climbed onto the old school bus with the rest of us.

"Of course," Ms. Frizzle said as we started off, "the best way to *find* a frog is to *be* a frog!" Suddenly we were spinning . . . and getting smaller. Then the old school bus hopped away like a bullfrog!

We hopped through the woods toward a fast-running creek.

"I'm not feeling too well!" Ralphie moaned as we took a bad bounce. "Could we stop, please?"

"What do you think, class?" asked Ms. Frizzle. "Should we start looking for Bella here?"

"This looks like a good frog habitat to me," Wanda said. "Lots of insects to eat, plenty of running water. Let's look!" Ms. Frizzle stopped the bus. "Everybody out!" she said.

We all looked around.

"Bella *must* be here," Wanda said, as she ran toward the stream.

"*Bella!*" she called.

Wanda didn't see Arnold, who was looking at some rocks. She tripped and . . . *ka-sploosh!* They both landed in the cold, fast-running water.

"Help!" yelled Arnold as he and Wanda were swept downstream.

"Oh, no! Here comes a waterfall!" cried Wanda.

Just then, Ms. Frizzle and the school bus calmly swam by. They scooped Wanda and Arnold into a big net.

The bus dropped Wanda and Arnold gently onto dry land.

"Whew," said Wanda. "The water in that stream is too fast, even for a frog!"

Ralphie shook his head. "If Bella laid eggs in that water, they'd be two miles downstream before you could say 'ribbit'!"

"Excellent!" said Ms. Frizzle. "Bullfrogs need to lay their eggs in quiet water. But where . . . ?"

Then something flew by that caught her eye.

Watch the birdie, class!

"Aha! It's a great blue heron!" said Ms. Frizzle. "Follow that bird!"

"A great blue heron?" said Arnold. "Why are we following a great blue heron?"

The Friz did not hear him. She was already marching off.

We hiked and hiked. Finally we arrived at a big pond.
"Just as I thought!" said Ms. Frizzle. "A beaver pond!"
"Wow!" said Arnold. "The water is nice and quiet here."

Carlos knew all about beavers. He had just read a book about them.

He said, "Beavers need a quiet pond to live in. So they make their own habitat! They build a dam across a stream. Slowly, the place fills up like a bathtub. It turns into a pond. Plants grow. Bugs come to live in and eat the plants. And the bugs are food for other hungry animals, like . . ."

"*Bella!*" Wanda yelled. "There she is!"

"She has everything she needs in her habitat," Arnold said. "Plenty of space, lots of insects to eat, quiet water to lay her eggs in, and lots of fresh air, too!"

"*And* a great blue heron about to eat her!" gasped Wanda. "Hold on, Bella, I'll save you!"

Before anyone could stop her, Wanda waded into the water.

Wait, Wanda!

Oh, no!

I can't look!

Wanda splashed toward the middle of the pond.
She reached Bella's lily pad at the same time
as the heron.
Hop! Plunk! Bella disappeared into the water.
"Help!" yelled Wanda as the heron's beak poked
toward her.

We saw the heron fly away. For a moment, we could not see Wanda. Then we heard a squishing sound and saw Wanda coming out of the pond.

"Are you all right?" Arnold asked.

"All right? I was *almost* a heron's lunch!" Wanda sputtered. "But where's Bella?"

Then Wanda saw Bella sitting on her lily pad—just as if nothing had happened.

"Bella!" Wanda exclaimed happily. "You're all right! You had better come home with me. You can't stay here, where a heron might eat you."

"Not necessarily, Wanda," said Ms. Frizzle. "A heron *might* eat Bella—*if* it could catch her!"

"Oh," said Wanda. "You mean, Bella has places where she can hide from the heron. I guess they are part of her habitat, too. But, at least back at school, she'd be safe. What about — ?"

Wanda was interrupted by a strange noise. "GAR-RUMP! HER-MAN!"

Bella had a friend! "HER-MAN!" he croaked.

"Oh, no," said Arnold. "We'll never get *two* frogs back to school!"

Wanda looked at Bella and her friend. "You're right, Arnold," Wanda said, as she waded out to Bella's lily pad.

"Bella," Wanda said, "you have everything you need right here. Quiet water, hiding places, food, space—and your new friend! I'm going to leave you here in the habitat you found."

"BEL-LUH!" croaked Bella.

Wanda walked back to us. We all climbed
onto the school bus.

Great trip!

When we got back to school, we put away Bella's things. Arnold was glad to be back. "Ahh!" he said. "My desk, a roof over my head, my lunch, and my milk. It feels good to be back in my own habitat!"

Wanda did not look so happy.

"You miss Bella, don't you?" said Arnold.
Wanda nodded.
Then we brought out something we had made
for her. It was the world's biggest toy bullfrog.
"Surprise!" we yelled.
Tim pressed a button.
"GAR-RUMP!" croaked the frog.
Wanda smiled.

"Thank you!" said Wanda, giving the frog a big hug. "I love it!"

"It doesn't need water, food, *or* fresh air," said Ms. Frizzle.

"And it won't jump out the window!" said Arnold.

Letters from Our Readers

(Editor's note: They will help you tell what is real and what is make-believe in this story.)

DEAR EDITOR:
   I'VE NEVER SEEN A TEACHER DRESS LIKE MS. FRIZZLE! ALSO, WHERE DID SHE GET THOSE SHOES?

   SIGNED,
   WHAT WILL SHE WEAR NEXT?

To Whom It May Concern:
   My school bus never shrinks to frog size, sprouts legs, and then hops through the woods!

   From,
   No Excitement in My Life

P.S. Now that I think of it, people can't shrink, either. For safety reasons, please tell your readers not to try sitting on a lily pad unless they are wearing approved flotation devices!

Dear Editor:
   Didn't you know that blue herons do not eat people? However, they do eat frogs, fish, salamanders, snakes, lizards, and shrimp.
      Your friend,
      You Can't Fool Me!

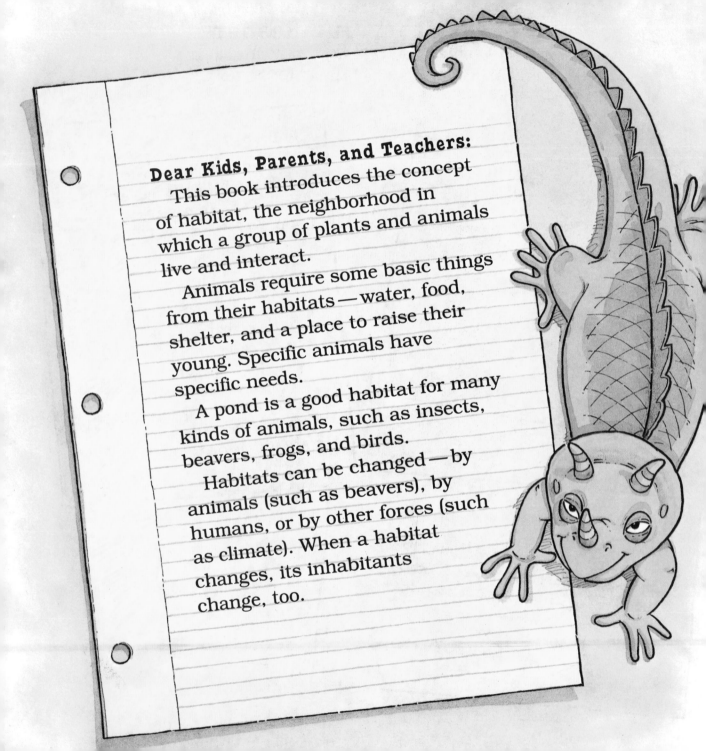

Dear Kids, Parents, and Teachers:

This book introduces the concept of habitat, the neighborhood in which a group of plants and animals live and interact.

Animals require some basic things from their habitats—water, food, shelter, and a place to raise their young. Specific animals have specific needs.

A pond is a good habitat for many kinds of animals, such as insects, beavers, frogs, and birds.

Habitats can be changed—by animals (such as beavers), by humans, or by other forces (such as climate). When a habitat changes, its inhabitants change, too.